DILLY
DINOSAUR SUPERSTAR

Stories of the World's Naughtiest Dinosaur

Tony Bradman

Rex came out of the record shop, and everyone started screaming. The dino-police had to hold back the crowd.

'Hi there,' said Rex. 'You must be the little dinosaur with the big voice.'

Dilly just stood there with a silly grin on his face.

Have you read all the **Dilly** books?

DILLY

DINOSAUR SUPERSTAR

Stories of the World's Naughtiest Dinosaur

Illustrated by Susan Hellard

MAMMOTH

First published in Great Britain 1989
by Piccadilly Press Ltd
Published 1991 by Mammoth
an imprint of Mandarin Paperbacks
Michelin House, 81 Fulham Road, London SW3 6RB

Mandarin is an imprint of the Octopus Publishing Group

Text copyright © Tony Bradman 1989
Illustrations copyright © Susan Hellard 1989

ISBN 0 7497 0431 4

A CIP catalogue record for this title
is available from the British Library

Printed in Great Britain
by Cox & Wyman Ltd, Reading, Berkshire

DILLY'S PET

'Father, can I have a pet?' asked Dilly one day.

'What, Dilly?' said Father.

It was a lovely, sunny morning, and we were all in the garden. Mother was basking in the sunshine, I was reading, Father was doing some gardening, and Dilly was supposed to be playing. But he was following Father around being a pest instead.

'All my friends have got pets,' said

Dilly. 'I'm the only one who hasn't.'

Dilly had caught up with Father in the part of the garden where the swamp roses grow. They're Father's favourite flowers, and he spends ages looking after them.

Father's always telling us about the little creatures which come into the garden to eat his plants. He says there's one in particular which just loves swamp roses. It's called a Swamp Lizard, and if we ever find one in the garden, we're

supposed to tell him.

'I'm sorry, Dilly,' he said, 'but your mother and I don't think you're ready to have a pet just yet.'

'But I *am* ready, Father,' said Dilly. 'I've been ready for ages!'

'What I mean, Dilly,' said Father with a sigh, 'is that you're not old enough yet. Pets can be hard work. You have to make them somewhere to live, remember to feed them regularly and maybe even take them for walks. We think you'd probably forget to do all that.'

'But I wouldn't, Father!' said Dilly. 'I *promise* I wouldn't!'

'I'm sorry, Dilly,' said Father. 'The answer is still no. You'll just have to wait until you're older.'

'It's not fair!' shouted Dilly. 'I want a pet and I'm going to have one!' He stamped his foot, and swished his tail around, and for a second I thought he was going to have a tantrum. Father was beginning to look angry, too. Luckily, Mother came to the rescue.

'It's such a lovely day,' she said quickly. 'Why don't we all go swamp wallowing?'

Dilly soon changed his tune. He loves swamp wallowing, and he couldn't wait to go. But if Mother and Father thought he'd forgotten about having a pet, they were wrong, as we found out later . . .

The next morning, I went with Father to the Shopping Cavern to buy a new pair of shoes for school. When we got home, Mother was cooking lunch and Dilly was playing in the garden. I took the lid off the box and showed Mother my new shoes.

'They're perfect, Dorla,' she said. 'Why don't you show them to Dilly? You

can tell him his toasted fern stalks are
ready, too.'

I went into the garden, and at first
I couldn't see Dilly. Then I saw his tail
sticking out from behind the giant fern.
He seemed to be kneeling down and
looking at something on the ground.
I couldn't see what it was.

'What *are* you doing, Dilly?' I said.

Dilly jumped and looked round at me.
He stood up, but I noticed that he kept
both paws behind his back.

5

'Nothing,' he said. I didn't believe him, though. He had his I-Know-I'm-Doing-Something-Wrong-But-I-Don't-Care look on his face.

I told him that lunch was ready, and showed him my new shoes in the box. I thought he'd say 'Yuck!' or 'They're stupid!' like he usually does, but he didn't. In fact he didn't really look at them. He was interested in something else.

'Can I have the box?' he said. '*Please*, Dorla?'

I was so surprised he'd said 'please' that I took the shoes out and gave him the box right there and then. We went back into the house, and Dilly ran upstairs.

'Dilly!' called Mother. 'Where are you going? Your lunch is on the table!'

'Coming, Mother,' Dilly called out. He came back downstairs and sat at the table. He didn't have the shoe box with him.

Dilly was very quiet and well behaved at lunch. As you know, he usually makes a real mess with his food, and he often spills his pineapple juice. But today he didn't do any of that, although he *was* rather slow. In fact, when everyone else had finished, Dilly's plate looked as if he'd hardly started.

Father told him he'd have to hurry up and finish while the rest of us tidied our dishes away.

'I will, Father,' said Dilly. And he did, too. The moment Mother, Father and I went out of the dining room and into the kitchen, he must have speeded up a lot. For when we came back, Dilly's plate was completely empty, and he was sitting there with a big smile on his face.

'Well, Dilly,' said Father. He looked

rather surprised. 'You must have been hungry after all.'

Dilly went up to his room after that, but he didn't stay in there for very long. After a while, there was a knock on my door. I opened it, and Dilly was standing there. He gave me a big smile.

'Can I *please* borrow some of your doll's house furniture, Dorla?' he asked, very politely. 'I promise I won't break it.'

Usually I won't let Dilly near my doll's house. But he'd asked so nicely, I couldn't really say no, especially as I could see Mother standing on the stairs listening. I let him choose what he wanted, and then he went back to his room.

Mother said it was nice to see Dilly being well behaved for a change. I didn't say anything.

That's because I was sure he was up to something.

I was even more sure of it later when he did something very strange. He came downstairs with the shoe box and asked Mother if he could go into the garden. She said he could. He went outside, marched round the garden twice, came back inside, and went straight up to his room. He looked really happy.

I kept my eye on Dilly all evening, but I couldn't work out what he was doing.

The next day, Dilly asked Mother if he could go into the garden again. He had the shoe box with him, and he kept looking at it. He seemed a little worried.

'Of course you can, Dilly,' said Mother. Dilly hurried outside, and I didn't think any more about it.

A little later, Father said he was going to do some gardening. He hadn't been outside long when we heard him call out. Mother and I went into the garden. Father was standing in the part where the swamp roses grow. He looked rather upset.

'They're gone,' he said. 'Every last one of them!'

It was true. The stalks had been stripped bare. Then I noticed a petal lying on the ground, and another, and another . . . They made a trail which led us to the giant fern. We went round

behind it, and there was Dilly with his
shoe box.

'Dilly,' said Father, 'I think you'd
better show me what's in the box.'

Dilly didn't say anything. He just
stopped smiling and held on to the box
more tightly.

'Come on, Dilly,' said Father. 'Hand it
over.'

Dilly didn't hand it over. Instead, he

blasted our ears with an ultra-special, 150-mile-per-hour super-scream, the sort that sends us all diving for cover behind the nearest fern bush.

We soon discovered what it was all about once Dilly had calmed down. Inside the shoe box was a Swamp Lizard he had found and made into his pet. He'd wanted my shoe box and doll's house furniture to make it a home, and all that marching round the garden had been to give his pet a walk.

He hadn't eaten his lunch the day before, either. He'd slipped it into a pocket for his pet when we weren't looking. The lizard had drunk some pineapple juice, but hadn't touched any of the toasted fern stalks. Dilly had been worried he would starve. Then he'd remembered that there was a flower Swamp Lizards just loved to eat . . .

Of course, Father was very cross. Dilly was told off and sent to his room for the rest of the day.

Later, at bedtime, I heard Dilly say he was sorry. He also asked Father if he could keep the Swamp Lizard.

'I did all the things you said, Father. So I must be ready to have a pet.'

'I'll think about it,' said Father. Then he sighed. '*You* might be ready, Dilly – but I'm not sure if *I* am yet . . .'

DILLY — DINOSAUR SUPERSTAR

'Dilly, will you *please* stop making that
horrible noise!' shouted Mother from
downstairs. She sounded very cross.
'I can hardly hear myself think!'

It was even worse for me. I was in my
room, which is right next to Dilly's. The
noise was so bad it was beginning to make
my teeth hurt and my tail twist. And he'd
been doing it all afternoon.

Dilly couldn't have heard Mother,
because the next thing I knew, she'd

come upstairs and was banging on his bedroom door. I went out on the landing. After a while, the noise stopped and Dilly's door opened.

'What on earth are you doing, Dilly?' said Mother.

'I'm only playing a game, Mother,' he said.

'Well, can't you play it more quietly? What sort of game is it, anyway?'

'I'm playing Rex and the Rockosaurs, Mother,' said Dilly with his biggest smile. 'I'm Rex – do you like my guitar?'

I hadn't noticed before, but Dilly was holding Father's old tennis racquet just like it was a guitar. He was also wearing some funny clothes from the dressing-up box – an old, shiny top of Mother's, and a scarf all covered in spangly stars. He had a pair of toy sun-glasses on, too.

I should have realised, of course. Recently, Dilly's done nothing but talk about Rex and the Rockosaurs. I like them too, and Dilly only started being a fan of theirs to copy me. But now he thinks they're wonderful. Whenever they're on the TV, he loves to sing along with them and dance in front of the screen so that no one else can see anything.

'Very nice, Dilly,' said Mother, with a sigh. 'But why don't you stop being Rex for a while and come downstairs for a snack? You can have your favourite if you like – a swamp-worm and swamp-nut butter sandwich with a glass of pineapple juice. How does that sound?'

Dilly said it sounded terrific. But he also said he didn't want to stop being Rex, so he kept his pop star outfit on while he ate and drank.

'You know, Mother,' he said between mouthfuls, 'one day I'm going to be a superstar on TV, like Rex and the Rockosaurs.'

'I'm sure you will be, Dilly,' said Mother. 'You make enough noise for a superstar, anyway. But for now I'd like you to concentrate on being a careful little dinosaur. I'm sure Rex doesn't spill pineapple juice down *his* front.'

That evening, Rex and the Rockosaurs were on TV again. They had made a new record called *Rock Around the Swamp*, and Dilly thought it was fantastic.

'Can we get it, Mother?' he said. 'Can we? Can we?' He bounced up and down in front of her so much that his dark glasses almost fell off.

'Well, Dilly . . .' said Mother, 'I don't know about that. It's only well-behaved, *quiet* little dinosaurs who get records bought for them.'

'I promise I'll be quiet, Mother,' said Dilly. He had his I'll-Be-As-Good-As-I-Possibly-Can look on his face.

'OK, Dilly,' said Mother. 'We'll buy it at the Shopping Cavern on Saturday. Dorla, you can have a record too.'

Dilly jumped up and shouted 'Hurray!' as loudly as he could, then remembered that he was supposed to be quiet.

'Sorry, Mother,' he whispered.

18

'That's all right, Dilly,' Mother whispered back, with a smile.

We set out in the dino-car early on Saturday morning. It's always crowded at the Shopping Cavern, and sometimes it's difficult to find a parking space. But when we arrived, we soon realised it was more crowded than we'd ever seen it before.

We got stuck in a traffic jam, and then there didn't seem to be anywhere to park at all. We found a space at last, and went into the Shopping Cavern. It was packed. There were dinosaurs coming from

19

everywhere, and they all seemed to be heading in one direction.

'What's going on?' said Mother.

'I don't know,' said Father. 'But if we want to get to the record shop, we'll have to follow everyone else. It's over there.'

Father pointed to where the dinosaurs were packed tightest. We joined the crowd and set off towards the record shop. It was hot, it was noisy, and everyone was pushing and shoving. Somebody even stood on my tail. After ten minutes we'd hardly got any nearer.

'This is ridiculous,' said Mother. She didn't look as if she was enjoying her trip to the Shopping Cavern one little bit. 'We'll never get there at this rate.'

Dilly looked upset. He'd gone bright green and his bottom lip had started to quiver, the way it always does when he's just about to cry.

'Does that mean I won't get my Rex and the Rockosaurs record?' he said.

Mother was just about to answer him when someone interrupted her. It was a teenage dinosaur who was in the crowd just in front of us.

'So you're a Rex and the Rockosaurs fan too,' she said to Dilly. 'I can't wait to see them . . . isn't this exciting!'

'You mean Rex and the Rockosaurs are *here*?' said Father.

'*Of course* they are,' said the teenager. 'Didn't you know? They're making a personal appearance at the record shop today to sign copies of their new single. There are TV cameras here, and everything.'

'Now we know why it's so crowded,' said Mother. She didn't look very pleased, but Dilly was absolutely delighted.

'I'm going to see Rex! I'm going to see Rex!' he kept saying. He was so happy and excited that he couldn't keep still. He pulled his dark glasses out of his coat pocket and put them on. 'Come on, Mother! *Let's go*!'

'I don't think we're going anywhere,' said Mother. 'This is impossible, Dilly. We'll have to come back another day.'

Dilly's face changed instantly.

'But I want to see Rex and the Rockosaurs, Mother,' he said.

'I'm sorry, Dilly,' said Mother, 'but I'm getting a headache, and I think we ought to go back to the dino-car.'

Dilly didn't say anything . . . he just opened his mouth and fired off an ultra-special, 150-mile-per-hour super-scream, the kind that makes a huge, noisy crowd of dinosaurs go very, very quiet all of a sudden.

Mother and Father were embarrassed, and tried to calm Dilly down, but he just wouldn't shut up. He screamed, and screamed, and screamed, and soon everyone was looking at him. After a while, a dinosaur pushed through the crowd and came up to us.

'Excuse me,' he said. Mother looked round. 'My name is Ronnie, and I'm Rex's manager. Rex was so impressed by your little dinosaur's voice that he'd like to meet him . . .'

Of course, Dilly stopped screaming *immediately*.

'Can I, Mother?' he said. 'Can I? Can I?'

At first I thought Mother wouldn't let him because he'd been so naughty. But in the end, she said it was OK. In fact, we all got to meet Rex. He came out of the record shop, and everyone started

screaming. The dino-police had to hold
back the crowd.

'Hi there,' said Rex. 'You must be the
little dinosaur with the big voice.'

Dilly just stood there with a silly grin
on his face. Then Rex asked him what he
wanted to be when he grew up, and Dilly
said he wanted to be a superstar. Rex
laughed.

'Come and see me in a few years,' he said. 'If you can sing as loud as you can scream, then I might just have a job for you in the Rockosaurs . . .'

Rex's manager gave us a signed record, and then they had to go. They got into the longest dino-car I've ever seen, and Rex waved to us as they drove off.

At bedtime that night, Dilly couldn't stop talking about what had happened. Finally he asked Mother if she thought Rex had really meant it about having a job for him. Mother said she was sure he had.

'Great!' shouted Dilly. 'I'm going to practise singing as loud as I can *every day* until then. Won't that be fun?'

Mother didn't say anything. But from the look on her face I could tell she didn't think it would be . . .

DILLY GETS JEALOUS

Now if there's one thing you can say about Dilly, it's that he doesn't like anyone else interfering with *his* things.

Take the other day, for instance. Dilly was playing with a toy he got for his birthday, a Magic Eggshell. It has lots of different parts, and if you move them in the right ways it turns into a dino-car, a robot or a spaceship.

But Dilly hadn't been able to work out how to do it yet. So when I say he was playing with it, what I mean is that he was *trying* to play with it, but only getting more and more cross. In the end, he stood up, stamped his foot, and threw the toy down as hard as he could.

I went over and picked it up. I only wanted to help him, but I never got the chance. Dilly grabbed the Magic Eggshell and pushed me away.

'You leave that alone, smelly old Dorla!' he shouted at me. 'It's *mine*, and you're not allowed to touch it!' He opened his mouth, and for a second I thought he was going to do what he usually does when he loses his temper . . . but just then, Father came through the door.

'Now, now, you two, what's going on?' said Father.

'I was only trying to help him with his toy, Father,' I said. 'He can't do it and it's making him cross.'

'It's *mine*, and I don't want any help!' shouted Dilly. Then he stuck his tongue out at me.

Father looked up towards the ceiling.

'Sometimes, Dilly,' he said with a sigh, 'I just don't know what I'm going to do with you. You're really going to have to learn to be a little less possessive.'

'What does poss . . . pess . . . what does that word mean, Father?' said Dilly.

'It means being a horrible little dinosaur who never lets anybody touch his things, even when they just want to help or be friends,' said Father. 'If you want others to be nice to you, Dilly, you've got to be nice to them. Now you go up to your room and think about it until lunch.'

Dilly came down a little later and said he was sorry. I knew why – Father had promised to take us to the park that afternoon, and Dilly didn't want to miss out on something he loves doing.

Father said he was forgiven, and we went to the park straight after lunch. I took my roller skates, and Dilly took his dino-trike. But he also insisted on bringing his Magic Eggshell along.

It was fun at the park. Dilly was on his best behaviour. We raced up and down on the track, and for once he didn't try to knock me over. After a while, we asked Father if we could go on the tree swings and the rock slide. He said we could, and also that he would look after my roller skates, and Dilly's dino-trike and Magic Eggshell.

'Hey, look!' said Dilly as we ran over to the swings. 'There's Dixie!'

Now as you probably know, Dixie is Dilly's best friend. He just loves playing with her, and I could see he was really pleased she was there. He ran over to her and started bouncing up and down the way he always does when he's excited.

'Hi, Dixie!' he said. 'What shall we play? I've got a great idea . . .'

Dixie didn't let him finish.

'I'm sorry, Dilly,' she said with a smile,

'but I can't play with you today. I'm playing with my *new* friend, Darryl.'

Dilly hadn't noticed the other little dinosaur who was standing just behind Dixie. But when he did, he didn't look very happy any more.

'But you're *my* friend, Dixie,' he said. 'And I want to play with you.'

Dixie didn't say anything. She gave Dilly a funny look, then ran off to the rock slide with Darryl.

Father went over to talk to Dixie's mother, and I had a long go on a tree swing. I was having such a good time that I didn't think about Dilly at all for a while. But when I got off the swing, I saw that he was standing by the rock slide.

Dixie was going up the steps. Darryl was about to follow her, but Dilly got in first. He pushed Darryl aside, and went up behind Dixie. I could see that he was talking to her. But she didn't say anything to him. She just went down the slide and waited for Darryl. Then they ran off together to the fern bush maze.

Dilly didn't give up, though. He followed Dixie and Darryl round the whole playground. He made lots of noise, and did all sorts of silly things to try and

make Dixie look at him. He even stood
on his head in the sandpit, and got
covered in sand from the top of his head
to the tip of his tail.

All the little dinosaurs in the
playground laughed at him and thought
he was really funny. All of them, that is
. . . except Dixie. She just wasn't
interested.

I could see that all this was making Dilly more and more cross.

Things went from bad to worse after that. Dilly still followed Dixie and Darryl around. But now he took every chance he could to get in Darryl's way. And then, by the roundabout, he even tried to trip him up.

'Dilly!' shouted Father. 'Come here at once!'

Dilly came stomping over, STOMP, STOMP, STOMP. He was looking very sulky.

'I saw that, Dilly,' said Father, 'and it wasn't very nice. If I've told you once, I've told you a thousand times – you are *not* to do that sort of thing. It can be very dangerous in a playground. You're lucky that little dinosaur was quick enough to get out of your way. And why are you being so horrible to him? He hasn't done anything to you, has he?'

Dilly didn't say anything. He just stood in front of Father with his I-Feel-Really-Mean-And-Nasty scowl on his face. Father was beginning to look quite cross.

'I think Dilly's jealous of him, Father,' I said.

'I am not!' shouted Dilly, but I took no notice.

'Dilly wants to play with Dixie, but she's playing with that little dinosaur,' I said. 'He's her new friend.'

'Well, Dilly,' said Father, 'you can't make someone play with you if they don't want to. You'll have to learn that being possessive with your friends is the quickest way to lose them.'

Father made Dilly sit on the bench next to him, and said he had to play with his Magic Eggshell. I wasn't sure if that was a good idea. He was still really sulky, and he just couldn't make it work. It wasn't long before he was looking even more cross than ever.

So you can probably guess what happened next.

That's right – Dilly threw down his Magic Eggshell as hard as he could, opened his mouth, and let rip with an ultra-special, 150-mile-per-hour super-scream, the sort that makes all the other little dinosaurs in the playground stop what they're doing and look at him.

Dilly calmed down at last. Father was in the middle of telling him off when Dixie and Darryl came over.

'Is Dilly all right?' asked Dixie.

'I think so, Dixie,' said Father. 'He's just being silly because he can't make his toy work.'

'Is it a Magic Eggshell? I've got one of those,' said Darryl. Before Dilly could say a word, Darryl picked up the Eggshell, and with three quick flicks, he turned it into a dino-car, then a robot, and then a spaceship. Dilly just looked at him in amazement.

'How did you do that?' he said.

'It's easy when you know how,' said Darryl. 'I'll show you if you like . . .'

Dilly sat quietly while Darryl taught him how to make the Eggshell work. After a few minutes the two of them looked as if they'd always been the best of friends. Dilly, Darryl and Dixie played together for the rest of the afternoon.

On the way home, Father said he was pleased that Dilly had learned not to be so possessive and liked Dixie's new friend.

'But he's not Dixie's friend, Father,' said Dilly. 'Darryl is *my* friend.'

Father gave Dilly a hard look. For a second I thought he was going to tell him off again. But he didn't.

He just sighed

DILLY AND THE MINDER

The other morning, the post-dinosaur
brought Mother an important-looking
letter. It was good news. Mother had got
the job she'd applied for, and she was
very pleased.

Dilly didn't really understand, so
Mother had to do some explaining. She
told him about how she'd given up work
when I was born so she could take care of
me. Father had been the one who earned
the money we needed.

'Then *you* were born, Dilly,' she said,
'and I had two little dinosaurs to look
after. But I always wanted to go back to
work one day, and now I can. The extra
money will help, too.'

I could see that Dilly was thinking very
hard about all this.

'But if you go to work, Mother,' he
said, 'who's going to look after . . . *me*?'

Mother gave Dilly a hug, and told him
not to worry.

'We've thought about that, Dilly,' she
said. 'I won't be going to work every day,
and you'll be at nursery school most of
the time, anyway. But when you're not,
you can go to a minder. You remember
what a minder is, Dilly – it's someone
who looks after little dinosaurs when
their parents go to work. We've already
found one for you. Her name is Mrs Dolf,
and she lives just around the corner.'

'But I don't want to be looked after by a stupid old minder,' said Dilly, and stamped his foot. 'I only want to be looked after by . . . YOU!'

'There's no need to shout, Dilly,' said Mother. I could see that she was trying to be patient. 'It won't be so bad. I'm sure you'll enjoy it.'

Dilly opened his mouth, and for a second I thought he was going to do what he usually does when he gets cross about something. But he didn't get the chance.

'Is that the time?' said Father suddenly, looking at his watch. 'I'd better hurry, or I'll be late for work!'

Mother said I'd be late for school, too, so we all started rushing around. All of us, that is, except Dilly, who just sat at the breakfast table with a strange look on his face . . .

That evening, Mother and Father tried

very hard to get Dilly used to the idea of going to a minder. But nothing seemed to work. They told him he wouldn't be there long, that Mrs Dolf had lots of toys for him to play with and books to read, and that she might even take him to the park sometimes – if he were a good little dinosaur.

Dilly didn't say anything. He just sulked.

'I'll take you to meet her tomorrow, Dilly,' said Mother. 'You can meet Danni, too. That's Mrs Dolf's little dinosaur . . . I think he's a bit older than you. So you'll have someone to play with. That will be nice, won't it?'

'No, it won't,' said Dilly. He stamped off upstairs to his room, STAMP, STAMP, STAMP, with his I'm-Going-To-Sulk-As-Hard-As-I-Can look on his face. Then he slammed his bedroom door behind him – SLAM!

Father told him off for being naughty, and said he had to stay in his room until bedtime.

The next morning, Mother took Dilly round to meet Mrs Dolf. When I got home from school, Dilly was upstairs in his room, and Mother was looking very cross.

The visit hadn't been a success. Dilly

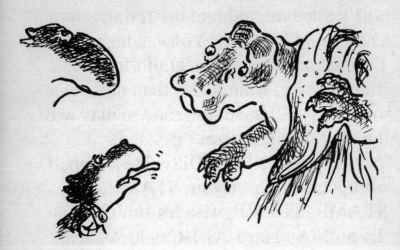

had stuck his tongue out at Mrs Dolf
and called her a rude name. Then he'd
thrown a tantrum, swished his tail around
and knocked over a vase with a fern plant
in it. The vase was smashed to pieces, and
there had been a terrible mess on the rug.

Mrs Dolf had been very nice about it,
and Mother said Danni had laughed.
I guess he thought it was funny. But
Mother didn't, and when she got Dilly

home, she had told him off and sent him to his room for the rest of the day.

He came downstairs for dinner later, and said he was sorry. Mother said he would have to be much better behaved the next time they went to Mrs Dolf's, and that he would also have to save up his pocket money to pay for a new vase.

Dilly looked very thoughtful. He didn't say much more, except to ask Mother if she thought Danni had been laughing at *him*.

'He might have been, Dilly,' said Mother. 'You do look pretty silly when you're misbehaving like that.'

After that, Dilly was very quiet.

The rest of the week went quite quickly, and it wasn't long before Mother's first day at work came round.

She got up very early and spent a lot of time getting ready. She put on the new

clothes she'd bought especially for her
job. Father and I said she looked terrific.
Dilly didn't say anything.

Soon it was time for everyone to go.
Mother was going to take me to school on
her way to work. That was the easy part.

But first we had to drop Dilly off at
Mrs Dolf's.

'Come on, Dilly,' said Mother. 'Put
your coat on. We haven't got much time.'

Dilly just crossed his arms and stared very hard at her.

'I hope you're not going to be naughty, Dilly,' said Mother. 'That's the last thing I need today.' It was true. I could see she was feeling nervous enough about starting her new job without worrying about Dilly.

He still wouldn't put his coat on, though. Mother had to do it for him. He didn't help her at all. He held his arms as stiffly as he could, which made it really hard work.

'Right,' said Mother at last. She was out of breath and all green in the face. 'We're ready . . . Off we go!'

But Dilly still didn't budge. He had his I'm-Going-To-Be-As-Stubborn-As-I-Can look on his face, and that *always* means trouble.

In the end, Mother had to drag him out of the house, up the path, through the gate and along the street. Just as we were going round the corner, he grabbed hold of a fern bush and wouldn't let go.

Mother pulled and pulled, and I pulled too, and finally we managed to tear Dilly away and arrive at Mrs Dolf's front door. Mother rang the bell, the door opened, and there was a lady dinosaur with a nice face. A small dinosaur a little bigger than Dilly peeked round from behind her. That must be Danni, I thought.

'Hello, Dilly!' said Mrs Dolf. 'It's nice to see you again. Why don't you come in?'

Dilly didn't say anything. He just stood there, looking at Danni.

'I'm afraid Dilly's being a little awkward this morning, Mrs Dolf,' Mother said.

'I don't believe it,' said Mrs Dolf with a big smile. 'He'll be all right once he's come in and settled down, won't you, Dilly?'

I looked at Dilly. I was so sure he was going to scream that I had my paws over my ears already.

But he didn't. Instead, he marched straight into Mrs Dolf's house, keeping his eyes on Danni all the time. He didn't look at Mother at all, or say goodbye to her. She seemed quite upset.

'Are you sure?' she said, anxiously.

Mrs Dolf said she was. So we left, but as we walked away, I thought Mother looked as if she were going to cry.

She needn't have worried, though. When we went to pick Dilly up later, everything was fine. Mrs Dolf said he'd been a little quiet at first, so she'd had a talk with him. It turned out that he was more worried about Danni than her or being in a strange house. But Danni showed Dilly all his toys, and the two of them had soon made friends. They were playing happily together when we arrived.

In fact, Dilly was having such a wonderful time he didn't want to leave.

'Come on, Dilly,' said Mother. 'It's time to go home.'

Dilly stamped his foot, opened his mouth, and . . . that's right, you guessed it, he let rip with an ultra-special, 150-mile-per-hour super-scream, the kind that usually makes Mother cringe with embarrassment and want to hide under the nearest table.

But today she just smiled.

'For once, Dilly, I'm almost glad you don't want to do what you're told,' she said. 'I really am!'

DILLY THE DINOSAUR is the first title in the DILLY series

Dilly is the naughtiest dinosaur in the whole world.

There was the time he decided he wasn't ever going to wash again. Another day he decorated his bedroom using his sister's best painting set.

And when he *doesn't* get his way, he opens his mouth and lets loose his ultra-special, 150-mile-per-hour super-scream!

The second book in the DILLY THE DINOSAUR series is

DILLY'S MUDDY DAY

Have you heard about Dilly? He's the naughtiest dinosaur in the whole world. Especially when he doesn't get his own way.

Like the day when he went to the park and rode his dino-trike into the swamp. And the time he wanted more pocket money and tried to open his own shop . . .

*The third book in the DILLY THE
DINOSAUR series is*

DILLY TELLS THE TRUTH

You must know Dilly – he's the naughtiest dinosaur ever!

He's never out of trouble, even when he's trying to be *good*. Like the time he kept on telling the truth – although he really shouldn't have . . .

*The fourth book in the DILLY THE
DINOSAUR series is*

DILLY AND THE HORROR FILM

The naughtiest dinosaur in the world is staying with
granny for the evening. It's movie time! They both
get a fright when the late film turns out to be a
spooky one. Having a 150 mph scream can have its
problems . . .

MEET THE WORLD'S NAUGHTIEST DINOSAUR

Even though, as everyone knows, he's the world's naughtiest dinosaur Dilly still has lots of fans. Now that he is so famous he's started making special visits to bookshops to meet the people who enjoy reading about him. You might be able to meet him in your local bookshop – he usually tries to behave himself!

If you would like to meet Dilly yourself ask your teacher or your librarian to invite him to visit your school or library. The address to write to is written below. You can also write to this address for more information about Dilly and his books and about other books published by MAMMOTH.

MAMMOTH Press Office,
38 Hans Crescent,
London SW1X 0LZ

A Selected List of Fiction from Mammoth

While every effort is made to keep prices low, it is sometimes necessary to increase prices at short notice. Mammoth Books reserves the right to show new retail prices on covers which may differ from those previously advertised in the text or elsewhere.

The prices shown below were correct at the time of going to press.

☐	7497 0366 0	**Dilly the Dinosaur**	Tony Bradman	£1.99
☐	7497 0021 1	**Dilly and the Tiger**	Tony Bradman	£1.99
☐	7497 0137 4	**Flat Stanley**	Jeff Brown	£1.99
☐	7497 0048 3	**Friends and Brothers**	Dick King-Smith	£1.99
☐	7497 0054 8	**My Naughty Little Sister**	Dorothy Edwards	£1.99
☐	416 86550 X	**Cat Who Wanted to go Home**	Jill Tomlinson	£1.99
☐	7497 0166 8	**The Witch's Big Toe**	Ralph Wright	£1.99
☐	7497 0218 4	**Lucy Jane at the Ballet**	Susan Hampshire	£2.25
☐	416 03212 5	**I Don't Want To!**	Bel Mooney	£1.99
☐	7497 0030 0	**I Can't Find It!**	Bel Mooney	£1.99
☐	7497 0032 7	**The Bear Who Stood on His Head**	W. J. Corbett	£1.99
☐	416 10362 6	**Owl and Billy**	Martin Waddell	£1.75
☐	416 13822 5	**It's Abigail Again**	Moira Miller	£1.75
☐	7497 0031 9	**King Tubbitum and the Little Cook**	Margaret Ryan	£1.99
☐	7497 0041 6	**The Quiet Pirate**	Andrew Matthews	£1.99
☐	7497 0064 5	**Grump and the Hairy Mammoth**	Derek Sampson	£1.99

All these books are available at your bookshop or newsagent, or can be ordered direct from the publisher. Just tick the titles you want and fill in the form below.

Mandarin Paperbacks, Cash Sales Department, PO Box 11, Falmouth, Cornwall TR10 9EN.

Please send cheque or postal order, no currency, for purchase price quoted and allow the following for postage and packing:

UK 80p for the first book, 20p for each additional book ordered to a maximum charge of £2.00.

BFPO 80p for the first book, 20p for each additional book.

Overseas including Eire £1.50 for the first book, £1.00 for the second and 30p for each additional book thereafter.

NAME (Block letters) ....

ADDRESS ....

....

....